ISBN 13: 978-1942500605
ISBN 10: 1942500605

Boulevard Books
The New Face of Publishing
www.BoulevardBooks.org

Me, You and Him

by Lazarus

Prologue:

The poetry came so easy to me - it felt as if it was already written. It was a moment - intertwined in the illusion of time - where GOD spoke profoundly to me. The "coincidences" all made sense.
It was clear,... and I was ready,... so I saw...
and I listened.

Now a synopsis? I never planned to sit down to write the book itself in the first place.
How do I do this when it was GOD's Love that guided the pen the first time?
When will I be that inspired again?
When will my pursuit for the highest truths, and my path towards the greatest goods lead me to this Love once more?

And so I waited.. waiting for that touch of divine intervention. But in my waiting, I wasn't listening. I was waiting for something that is already with me....
       .... was always with me.....
       .... and will always be with me...

So why then can't I always feel it?
Hear it?
See it?

I kept waiting for it to be the same –
So profound that it couldn't be mistaken
for anything else.
Is that even fair?
I want it to always be that way –
is that wrong?
Or is that the eternal peace we speak about?
What if we ALL could hear it?
What if we ALL could hear it.... ALL the time?

I understand better now that I can see
GOD's love when I am being true,
and sharing good with someone else.
It's real easy to listen then.
And everything makes sense.

I want to always be ready to listen!
But sometimes I don't want to put in the work.
Sometimes I have my own plan,
GOD's love speaks to me,
but I listen to what I think I needed to hear.
It can be overwhelmingly confusing at times.
Sometimes I justify not listening with my suffering;
but then the justification becomes a part
of my suffering
Sometimes I see the love, but I walk blindly.
Sometimes I hear the Love, but then listen to the pain.
And sometimes I hear nothing at all....

.... and I feel lost.

It can be so dark.

But through GOD's love, a friend and teacher
of mine, once told me:
        "the quickest way to heaven
           is walking straight through hell."

And so as the Wise Men
brought a gift of the elements
to the son of GOD,
a chemistry student of mine
gifted me a booklet of sketches....
telling the story — from creation to salvation —
with this n_ote_... sprinkled in GOD's love:

This little booklet is from a guy
that came into my work and started
talking to me about this stuff, which
I thought you might consider to be
a sign.
                Merry Christmas
                and Enjoy!

                        - Gianna C. :)

She too-hungry for truth — shared GOD's Love
with me in her own pursuit of the transcendent within.
She felt my pain, and knew I needed healing.

Carelessly, I lost the booklet... I'm not the most
organized of individuals. Life has taught me that.
I learned how to lose what I had
because at any moment, you can lose everything.
I have sort of always let GOD's Love lead me —
but never truly acknowledging the strength of my faith.
But just as I was blind of the power of
the faith that I had lost,
I didn't even know I had lost the booklet....
.... until I found it.

It was the last day before Christmas break,
and I needed the time.
I was in between a series of five corrective surgeries
to mend chronic bone infections.
But it wasn't just my body —
my mind was clouded,
and my soul was tired.
And as with the trinity within me,
the booklet was worn & weathered too.
It was out in the cold December rain....
.... in a dark corner....
.... waiting for me to find it.

The moment itself - indescribable - but the feeling
I will never forget.
Tingling in GOD's goosebumps...
Maybe goosebumps is the feeling you get
when GOD hugs you?

I knew in that moment, where time seemed to
stand still...,
that I found more than just her gift.
It was meant for me....
it was a sign...
it was GOD's Love there to heal me.

I went home, dried out the booklet of sketches,
and the next morning - it was written.
My mind amid a myriad of metaphors, it felt
slightly out of body.
It helped immeasurably!
But I still write to you
with more healing to do.

And it wasn't me waiting for GOD -
it was GOD's Love waiting for me.
I also know now that GOD's Love is our gift to share.
He speaks to us - through each other -
in His image & likeness, so that we can talk about Him.
I can't do it on my own.
And so this work is an invitation by me -
Lazarus - to join in this shared experience of GOD's Love.
.... a part of "Me" I gift to "You"
        brought to me by You.....
                so that we can share His Love again.

Poetry: Lazarus

Cover Art: Bryanna Ackermann

Preface: Gianna Castano

Art/illustrations:

Page 1: Nicolette Figliozzi
Page 2: Corinne Kamien
Page 3: Catherine Nieves
Page 5: Tashi Mar
Pages 6 & 7: Bryanna Ackermann
Page 9: Sophia Pisano
Page 10: Tashi Mar
Page 11: Sabrina Ortiz
Page 13: Nicholas Andrianos
Pages 15 & 16 & 18: Corrine Kamien
Page 19: ???
Page 20: Alice Berte
Page 21: Corrine Kamien

PREFACE

The congregation of brilliant minds.
  The perceptions of them.
    That is what inspired this book.

      The coalition of ideas.
        The rumination of them.
          That is what set this book

in motion.

        The desire to be heard.
          The desire to spread the word.
            That is how this book came

to be.

The things in existence all began with an idea. This book is an empire of thoughts from adventurous, truth-thirsty students who have much to learn and look forward to in the years to come. The accumulated drive of the moderator and club members who devote their time to the growth of each other is what sparked the idea to create this book. This books' purpose is not to be published for money; it is to feed and fuel those who read it. As a body of thinkers, we encourage whoever reads this book to jot their own questions and comments all over.

Stay hungry for answers.

In the beginning it was **HIM** -
He faceless, us formless - perfect without **SIN**.
In all to be, His light energy....
perfect good, transcendent from **WITHIN**.

But **AMEN!** In a world — our breath birth from **trees** —
we've gone paper less, yet Knowledge grows on **these**.
So take advantage, and indulge my handwriting **please**...
for the sin begun, we no longer ONE — the story of
You, HIM, and **ME**.

So we ate from the **tree** when it was just you & **me**
Original Sin — disorder from within — as knowledge spread from **HE.**
The creation **mystery**...
and so in all matters that exist to **BE,**
HE, greater than the ONE as you and **me...,**

...built a wall - tall - HE without **sin** to lock us **in**
for it used to be so simple when it was just me, you, & **HIM**.
But for a second in time, learn from within, i see HIS **providence**
slow down the divine, perfect without sin, & live HIS **promises**.

So in time no longer ONE — me, you & HIM misunderstood —
dispersed energy and high entropy has taken us from good
Sin and suffering spread as would, imbalance grew faster than it begun
from you & me, to we — Earth, stars, daughters, and the Sun

And then we found more like us - in fact, we are all like us
the stench of sin and suffering sometimes seems like a must
We miss the me, you & HIM us - in true good we trust...
But sin's stench bearable in a crowd; so we don't shower much.

We found each other, but only because that's part of HIS plan to walk hand in hand, HIS WORD fruitful food for the wise man. We do all we can, when we submit to HIS command— but in sin, it's the fool leading liquor in hand.

But sin's stench aside, the sighs are so **visible**
and it seems like coincidences **match up**
More than one, and sometimes so **visceral**
to help lead us past sin's stench playing **catch up**.

With the fire in **view**, the signs are still there **too**...
we all found each other — now what shall we **do?**
God's love? Is that **new?** We'd like to start **anew** —
we still remember the time when it was me, HIM, and **you**

Hey look! Maybe it's *inside* — and no one is on *line*
And as I get closer, I feel a love in tune with *mine.*
We can't help but be **curious**, sin's stench is making us **furious**
Sin step aside, it's time! — maybe we need love to **experience?**

Let's keep following these signs, but this stench is still strong **though**
some now waiting on line, but guest list put everyone on, so...
ONE way to no wrong — the sin, we exist not as **ONE**
to confess this ... before and after HE was **born.**

But sin's stench is **persistent** - hmm... so this is art?
Let's talk to GOD. I get the *gist*... we remember **this**
But this dude... who's cross is **this?**
Arms spread wide and open heart? HIS strength seems odd!
We can do **this?** Back to when me, you, & HIM **exist?!**

Looks like this Jesus dude suffered to help us carry ours **within**
And maybe to bear our suffering is the teaching of all **religion**
And maybe if we don't begrudge each other we can return to
the **beginning**
And maybe it can be as good as the ONE when it was just
me, you, and **HIM.**

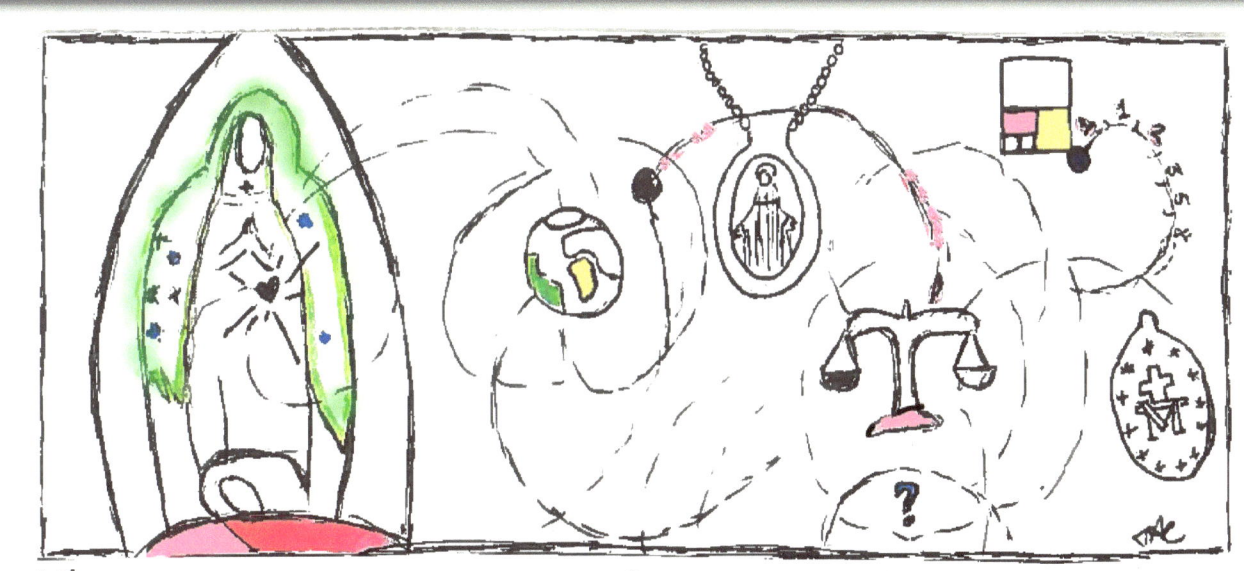

We miss me, you, and HIM — and sometimes it's within **HER**
And this LOVE reminds me of true good when things once **were**
And maybe it's not just in Him or **HER** — and this LOVE is in **them**.
And GOD is this collective conscious — of ALL things — beginning to **end**

And so LOVE through your suffering! A simple message to **send**
Live as ONE, and so less suffering if we choose LOVE over **sin**.
And so LOVE and live the prayers of others — hearts all **in**
S:☉ that we return to the harmony of ONE when it was just
me, you, & **HIM.**

His love is for real; but for some, hard to feel
But it's great! So be aware, because it's everywhere
God speaks so we can hear – our reality what we make real
we aren't suppose to bear the stench of despair.

But let's not be preachy - me and you have much **to learn.**
I think this JESUS dude can teach me - that stench was starting **to burn.**
Let me help you carry your cross...Look! Sin's stench is **gone**
And together we can't be lost if it's LOVE I carry you **on.**

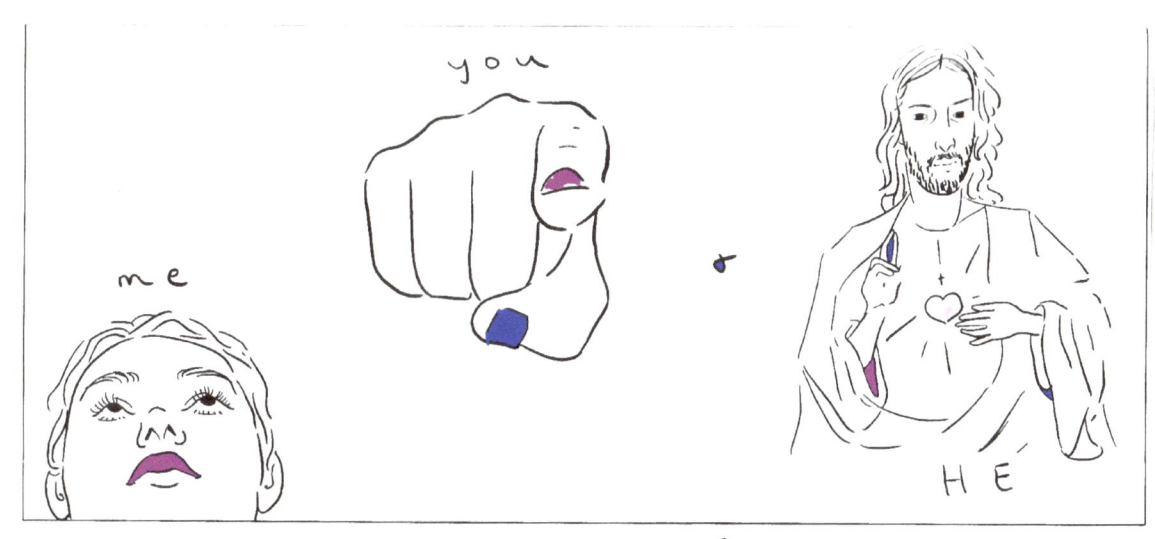

I think I can help you, and I think you can help **me**
And I think that's how it's got to **be**
to be me, you, i **HE** ooo
But I'm kind of new, so I'm going to do like this **J.C.**
let GOD judge the **we**
and unconditionally LOVE my **enemy**

But, wait! We all have a place here - comeback and stay for *awhile*
That apple - in all that we taste & fear - sometimes our hearts in *denial*
For sin's stench is so **vile**, and sometimes it's hard to learn **love**
But thankfully, after you leave here, another door will open from **above**

Sometimes sins stench is so strong even God's love smells wrong
The sin becomes ingrained within — we aimlessly wander along
But in time, there are times — follow the signs... remember HIS glow?
Maybe it's not mine I need to find — maybe it's GOD'S LOVE to help me grow

And so as some trickle in, and we choose LOVE over **sin**
In ONE we **win**... remember that? Way back **when**...
And we rise into **heaven**, but maybe not **in**...
... a literal sense - but in a sense, only with a **friend**,
and maybe it will be me, You, & HIM once **again!**

AMEN! HE brought a friend — the SON of **man?**
And there are others... all the same — coincidence **again?**
I think we understand.... let's choose LOVE over **sin**
And return to a time, harmony of ONE, when it was just me, you & **HIM!**

22

Some say I am the strongest person they know...
But my Mom is the strongest person I know!
Thank You Mother
I love You

Thank You to all of my family & friends –
old, new, past, present, and timeless....
Thank You to all my students for
inspiring me
Thanks to those who helped me remaster
the sketches & art we gift to you.
Thanks to those who helped heal me
along my pilgrimage
And thank you...
...those of you who have shared
God's love with me...
and helped shaped the
infinite Him
within me.
I need you to get back to Him.

Follow Lazarus on his journey....

... on Twitter @ProfessorLaz

....read along w/ Lazarus at

Soundcloud.com/professorLaz